1989

Eleanor Schick

A PIANO FOR JULIE

by Eleanor Schick

GREENWILLOW BOOKS NEW YORK

Library of Congress Cataloging in Publication Data
Schick, Eleanor, (date)
A piano for Julie.
Summary: Having heard "Someday we'll get
a piano" for a very long time, Julie is
delighted when someday really does come.
[1. Piano—Fiction] I. Title.
PZ7.S3445Pi 1984   [E]   83-14154
ISBN 0-688-01818-1
ISBN 0-688-01819-X (lib. bdg.)

FOR MARK,

AND FOR LEO

Sometimes, on Sundays,
we visit Grandma.
She still lives
on the same street,
in the same apartment house
where Daddy grew up.

Every time we visit Grandma,
after the tea and cake and talking
Daddy plays the piano.
It's the same piano Daddy played
when he was young, like me.
It's the one that Grandpa played.
I love to listen
as the music fills the room.
I listen, and I watch,
and I wish that I could learn
to make those magic sounds too.
Daddy always says, "Someday, Julie,
we'll get a piano too."
I want someday to come quickly.

One Sunday,
after we visited Grandma,
Mommy and Daddy
talked at the kitchen table
late into the night.
I heard Daddy say,
"It's time to buy a piano."

Every night since Sunday
when Daddy gets home from work,
he reads the For Sale ads
in the newspaper.
He says to me, "I'm looking
for a used piano, Julie.
I want to have one again!"
"I want us to have one too, Daddy.
I want to learn to play the piano!"

Every night Daddy makes phone calls,
asking about the pianos that
are for sale. Sometimes, after dinner,
he goes out to look at one.
Then one night Alice comes over
from next door to stay with me
so Mommy and Daddy can
go out together to see a piano.
When they come home, they say,
"We found it, Julie!
We found a fine piano.
The piano movers
will bring it on Saturday."

On Saturday, we get up early.
We move the bookcase
away from the living room wall.
We sweep the floor behind it.
We move the bookcase into the hall.
Now there's an empty wall
in the living room
where the piano will be.

We wait all day
for the piano movers to come.
Daddy takes an old cardboard box
down from the top of the closet.
It's filled with books of music
that are very old.
The pages are cracked and yellow.
Daddy tapes them carefully
where they are torn.
He shows me one.
"This was my first piano book, Julie.
Now it's yours.
My father taught me to play,
and I will teach you."

The doorbell rings.
It's the piano movers.
They roll the piano in
on a board with wheels.
They tilt it just the right way,
and put it against the wall
where the bookshelf used to be.

We have our piano!

I ask Daddy if I can play it.
"Of course," he says.
Daddy shows me where to sit.
The right place is the middle
of the piano bench
just far enough from the piano
to reach the keys.
He teaches me to play
"Twinkle, Twinkle, Little Star."

I play the notes
till I know them by heart.
I play them and play them
until my fingers hurt.
I want it to sound right.
And then it does!
It sounds like real music.
Daddy says, "You'll be
a fine musician, Julie!"
Mommy says, "You're playing
beautifully!"
We all go in to have our
very late, very happy dinner.

After dinner,
Daddy goes to the piano.
He dusts it
and cleans it everywhere.
He puts his music
in two neat stacks on top.
It's very late,
but no one says,
"It's bedtime, Julie,"
the way they always do.

Daddy sits down.
He closes his eyes.
He plays.
The music fills the room,
and the house,
and the night sky.
Somedays really do come.

The moon rises
in the corner of the window.
The music sounds like the moonlight.
Someday I will play that music too.